Pirouettes

Bootsie Barker
BALLERINA

story by **BARBARA BOTTNER**
pictures by **G. BRIAN KARAS**

HarperCollinsPublishers

HarperCollins®, ♣®, and I Can Read Book®
are trademarks of HarperCollins Publishers Inc.

BOOTSIE BARKER BALLERINA
Text copyright © 1997 by Barbara Bottner
Illustrations copyright © 1997 by G. Brian Karas
Printed in the U.S.A. All rights reserved.

Library of Congress Cataloging-in-Publication Data
Bottner, Barbara.
    Bootsie Barker ballerina / story by Barbara Bottner ; pictures by
G. Brian Karas.
        p.   cm. — (I can read book)
    Summary: Bernie and Lisa get even with Bootsie Barker, who is
terrorizing their ballet class.
    ISBN 0-06-027100-0. — ISBN 0-06-027101-9 (lib. bdg.)
    [1. Ballet dancing—Fiction.   2. Bullies—Fiction.]   I. Karas, G. Brian,
ill.   II. Title.   III. Series.
PZ7.B6586B1   1997   96-27259
[E]—dc20   CIP
                                                                      AC

1   2   3   4   5   6   7   8   9   10
❖
First Edition

For the sportsmen in my life,
Gerald, Irving, and Jeffrey
—B.B.

For Elaine Meyers
—G.B.K.

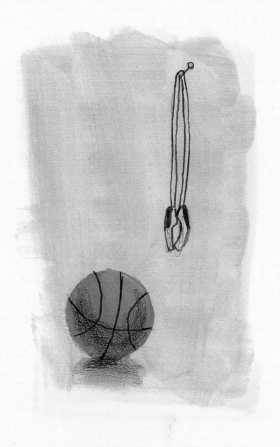

French Words in the Story

bonjour   *(bawn-ZHOOR)*   good morning, good day

madame   *(ma-DAM)*   Mrs., lady

monsieur   *(mes-YUH)*   Mr., sir

plié   *(plee-AY)*   bending the legs, with knees facing outward and the back held straight

relevé   *(reh-luh-VAY)*   rising up on the toes

pirouette   *(peer-a-WET)*   spinning on one foot

magnifique   *(ma-nyee-FEEK)*   splendid, magnificent

mademoiselle   *(mad-mwah-ZELL)*   miss, young lady

"Bernie," says Lisa. "You have to come to ballet class with me."

"Sorry. The guys are waiting."

"Please!" cries Lisa.

"You are just afraid that Bootsie Barker will be there," I say.

"I am NOT afraid of Bootsie Barker!" says Lisa.

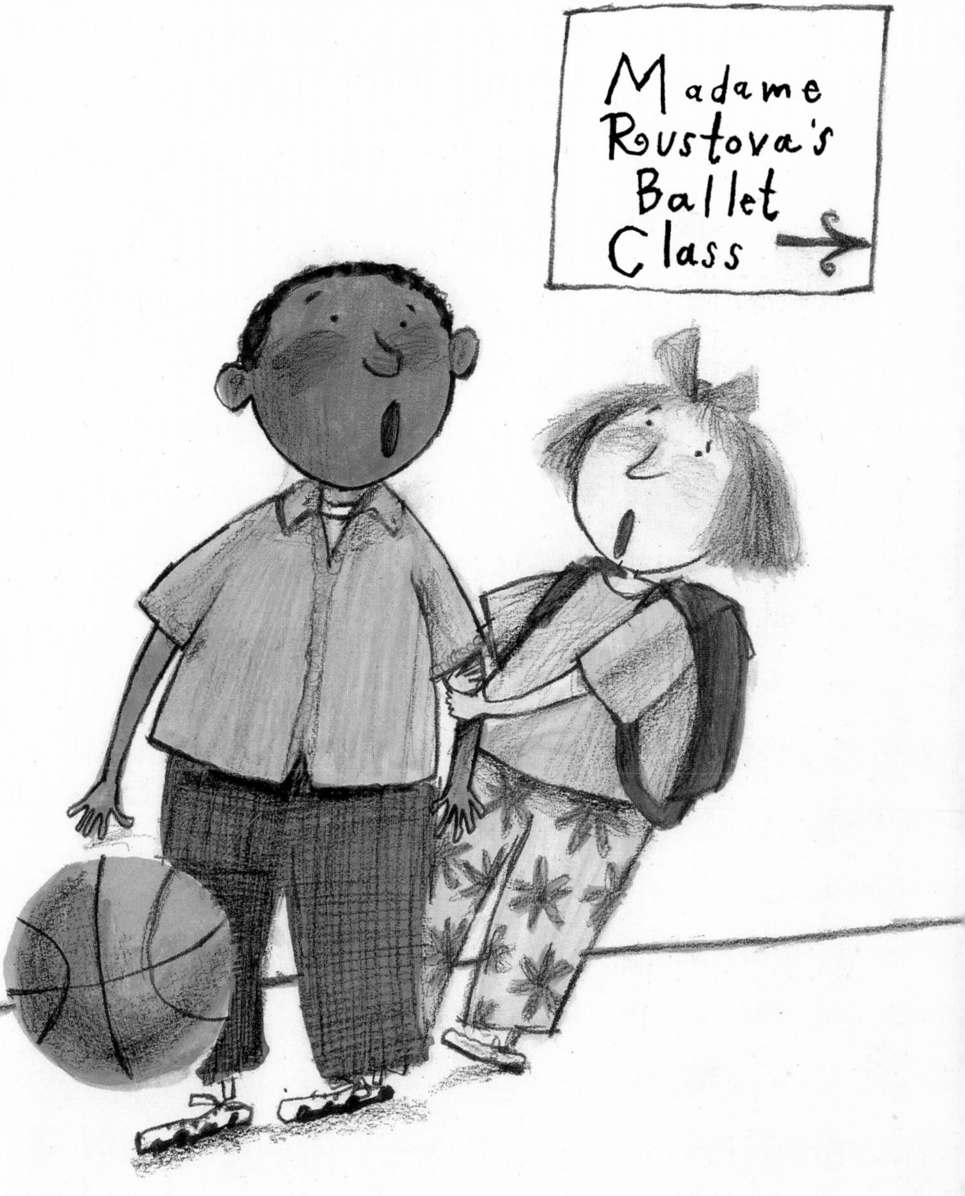
Madame
Rustova's
Ballet
Class

"Bonjour, Lisa," says Madame Rustova.

"And Monsieur Bernie! Our first boy!

And Bootsie Barker!

What a surprise to see *you* here!"

"Our Bootsie wants to learn

to be ladylike," says Mrs. Barker.

8

"I do *not*! I *hate* ballet," says Bootsie.

Then she looks at me.

"I hate boys even more!"

"I am sorry, Bernie," says Lisa,
"but Bootsie's mother sends her
wherever I go.
And now that Bootsie is here,
I want to go home."
"You can't," I tell her.
"You made me come here!"

Madame begins

with *pliés*.

"We must bend

like a frog,"

she says.

I smile at Lisa.

"I can do this,"

I say.

"*Anyone* can do this, stupid,"

says Bootsie Barker.

We all bend down.

Then we all get up—except Bootsie.

I feel something tugging at me.

It is Bootsie's arm!

I lose my balance
and fall into Lisa.
Lisa falls on Amy.
Amy falls on Kelly.

"Now *I* am the only one standing up," says Bootsie.

"That's not fair! You pushed Bernie," says Lisa.

"Be quiet!" says Bootsie.

"Ladies and gentlemen,

ballet dancers do *not* sit on the floor!"

Madame sounds just like my coach.

Later, I go to the gym.

"I am not any good at ballet,"

I tell Coach.

"Basketball players need to learn

how to keep their balance," he says

as he sinks a hook shot.

That night I dream

I dance Bootsie right off the stage.

"What a perfect dream,"

says Lisa when I tell her.

"Today, class, we will *relevé*,"

says Madame.

"Everyone float

like a tree in the breeze."

We all go up on our toes.

"This might help me

sink a jump shot," I say.

Then Bootsie trips me.

"*Ouch!* Why did you do that?" I ask.

"Boys do not float, knuckle knees."

Madame thinks Bootsie

is helping me up.

"Thank you, dear Bootsie,"

Madame says.

"Now, class, let us try to be birds."

"Want to fly, Nerdie Bernie?"

asks Bootsie.

When Madame looks away,

Bootsie grabs my wrist

and twists me around and around.

"You are one dead duck!"

"Stop!" Lisa screams.

"Lisa," says Madame, turning around,

"ballerinas *never* scream.

And Bernie, next time

please try to be a more careful bird."

Later I tell Coach, "I hate ballet class."

"Basketball players

are not quitters," he says.

That night I dream Bootsie is benched.

Forever.

"Today we will do *pirouettes,*"

says Madame.

"Across the floor in twos!"

Lisa and I spin

like tumbleweeds in the wind.

"*Magnifique!*" says Madame.

26

"Stinko!" says Bootsie. "Watch me!"

Bootsie spins, then falls.

"That boy made me dizzy!" she shouts.

"Oh dear," sighs Madame.

"Perhaps we are not ready for boys."

"But Bernie didn't do anything,"

says Lisa.

I ask Lisa to come with me

to talk to Coach.

28

"Coach, I am quitting ballet."

"But Bernie, it has

helped your game," Coach says.

"Coach is always right,"

I say as we walk home.

On our way to the next ballet class
we hear a thunderclap.
"There are two things I don't like—
thunderstorms and Bootsie Barker,"
says Lisa.
"Well, we can't stop the storm," I say,
"but maybe we can stop
Bootsie Barker."

"Class, today we will do

something different," says Madame.

"We will all make up

our own special dances."

"Okay! I am a gust of wind," I shout.

"And I am a hurricane!" shouts Lisa.

"Then I am the worst thing of all,"

Bootsie yells. "I am a tornado.

I WILL DESTROY EVERYTHING.

I WILL BLOW YOU AWAY!"

Bootsie twirls and twirls.

"Mademoiselle Barker," says Madame.

"Remember. Be graceful."

"Now, everyone, *dance*!"

Outside,

the rain plinks against the window.

"Lisa, follow me," I whisper.

We change directions.

Everyone follows us—

everyone but Bootsie.

She heads the wrong way

and crashes into Madame.

"You oaf!" snaps Madame.

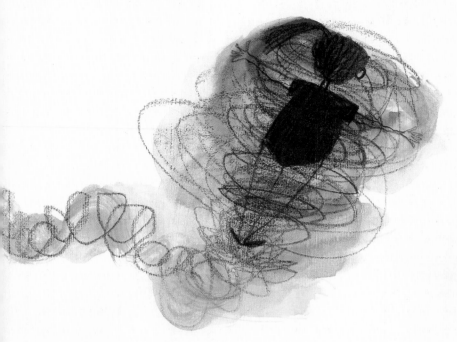

"Too bad, Madame," says Bootsie,

"but you were in my way."

"*You,* Mademoiselle Barker,

are *no* ballerina!"

Bootsie spins by in a blur.

"Faster," I yell. "Faster, faster, faster!"

I signal Lisa.

She opens the back door.

Bootsie leaps out into the pouring rain.

The wind whistles and roars

and slams the door shut.

Madame gives Lisa and me stars.

"Practice, practice, practice," she says.

"I will see you all next week."

"Let me *in*!" screams Bootsie.

But no one—except us—hears her.

Ballet class is over.